I0621531

Cuffley Capers

by

Brent Cheetham

Grosvenor House
Publishing Limited

All rights reserved
Copyright © Brent Cheetham, 2017

The right of Brent Cheetham to be identified as the author of this
work has been asserted in accordance with Section 78
of the Copyright, Designs and Patents Act 1988

The book cover picture is copyright to Brent Cheetham

This book is published by
Grosvenor House Publishing Ltd
Link House
140 The Broadway, Tolworth, Surrey, KT6 7HT
www.grosvenorhousepublishing.co.uk

This book is sold subject to the conditions that it shall not, by way of
trade or otherwise, be lent, resold, hired out or otherwise circulated
without the author's or publisher's prior consent in any form of binding or
cover other than that in which it is published and
without a similar condition including this condition being imposed
on the subsequent purchaser.

'All characters and events in this publication are fictitious and any
resemblance to actual persons living or dead is purely coincidental.'

A CIP record for this book
is available from the British Library

ISBN 978-1-78623-890-0

INTRODUCTION

Just a few words, for those of you who a brave enough to attempt to read this small book. This book of five small stories is based in and around the small Hertfordshire village of Cuffley. All the locations mentioned in the book are real and can still be seen today with the exception of the Cuffley Hotel, which has now been converted into a Tesco Express. None of the characters are real, and none of the names are real. All the stories are made up, but I wanted to catch the ethos of the place, which is a hard if not an impossible thing to do. So many folk go through life, without seeing the funny side of things, and pompous folk need to be taken down a peg or two. So many books on village life are either too serious or too twee, which precludes normal folk from reading them. With this book I hope to have broken the mould and only time will tell if I have been successful with my endeavours. Reading one short story a night should hopefully send the reader to sleep with a smile on his or her face. Finally the author can confirm that the water from Cuffley brook is quite safe, and does not send folks in the area mad, as has been suggested by some.

DEDICATION

I would like to thank Mrs Julie Cheeseman,
for her help and advice in writing this book,
particularly the first short Story

'The Salutary Lesson and the Perfect Woman'.

THE SALUTARY LESSON
AND
THE PERFECT WOMAN – 1.

M r Pilchard Rainham woke up late that morning; in fact so late, that the milkman and the paper-boy had already done their duty. This was unusual for Pilchard, as he was normally up promptly by 6 am and was very much a creature of habit. Pilchard was seen as a queer bird, who by day worked as a cataloguer at a large London auction house, and by night he had a permanent whim to dress up in flowery flamboyant shirts, which made him look like a cross between an extra in *Hawaii Five-0* and Quentin Crisp. He pulled his bed covers off, and to his amazement he found he still had his shirt and trousers on, but even worse, he still had his shoes and socks on. Pilchard mouth was as dry as the Sahara desert, and he craved for a glass of ice-cold water. What had happened last night? He recalled going to the pub to have a few drinks with the boys, but after that his mind went blank. Oh yes, he said to himself, he remembered that he had brought an engagement ring for Sybil, for he had intended to propose to her next weekend, Sybil was one posh classy bird, who he had only known for about three months, but he felt that at the age of twenty-nine it was about time he settled down. Indeed last night was to be his thirtieth birthday bash, down at the Cuffley Hotel.

He got up from his bed, in a most unstable fashion and walked down the stairs into his lounge. The first thing that stuck him was the empty Chinese takeaway boxes on the settee, whilst there were three plates on the floor. He said to himself why three plates and all those empty Chinese cartons, surely I did not eat that much Chinese last night? He stepped gingerly over the plates, without picking them up, for what was needed now was a glass of water, or a pint of ice-cold milk. He made his way to the kitchen only to be greeted by a picture that looked like the battle of the Somme. The sink and the draining board were full of more empty plates, cups, and plastic knives and forks, whilst the litterbin was overflowing with empty Chinese cartons, beer cans and bottles that had spilt out all over the floor. Ignoring the carnage for the moment he went straight for the fridge, screwed the top off a litre of milk, and drank half of it down all in one.

He turned round still holding what remained of the litre of milk and went back to the lounge to try and figure out what happened last night. He sat down on the settee, after pushing the empty Chinese cartons on to the floor with one sweep of his hand. He took a further swig out of the milk carton, and put it on the floor. He placed his head in his hands, trying to recall last night but nothing came back to him. Then the sound of passing traffic hit him, it sounded like all of Rommel's Panzer army was on the move outside his window. He got up and closed a small window, went back to the settee and sat down again, but the noise was still too much for him, so he put his hands to his ears to try and cut out the worst of it. And then a further noise was brought to his attention, it sounded like a dog growling. He removed his hands from his ears to try and work out what it was and where it was coming from. First he thought it was coming from outside, but after a while he could work out that the noise was closer to home. He moved his head back and forth, and at long last his directional antenna were able to locate the source of the noise, it appeared to come from behind him. He got up, kicked the milk carton and spilt the milk on the carpet by mistake whilst offering an expletive to the gods. He went round the back of the settee to view a half-naked man, in his socks and underpants fast asleep on the floor. He had no idea who he was, so he slapped him in the face.

The chap woke up and said, "Ah Pilchard, thanks for letting me doss down for the night".

The chap got up, found his trousers and his shirt, as he was laying on them, put them on and left the premises. Mr Pilchard Rainham was so gob smacked he never said a word.

THE SALUTARY LESSON
AND
THE PERFECT WOMAN – 2.

Mr Pilchard Rainham said to himself, I must have been treble 'cheese caked' last night as he looked at his Micky mouse watch, which showed the time was 11.30 am. Must get down to the pub, and apologize for anything I have said or have done wrong last night. He decided to have a bath first, but thought better of it as he still felt unsteady on his feet, and did not want to risk slipping over getting into or extricating himself from the bath. He decided a shower was the best option. However when he got into the shower he found that he had adjusted the heat control into a far too hot position, and had to jump out again, as his skin had turned bright red. He readjusted the showerhead to a more reasonable temperature, and jumped back in, but this time the noise of the shower, was like banging small nails into his head. He turned the power shower down, and managed to have a wash of sorts. He finished his ablutions, found a new pair of trousers and a new jacket. He swapped his keys, handkerchief and wallet to his new trousers. He checked the inside pocket of his jacket, found the box with the engagement ring and decided this time it would be safer to leave it at home. He opened his sock draw and hid the box with the engagement ring in one of his socks.

Pilchard went back to the bathroom, put some bay rum on his hair, and combed it in. He then went back to his massive wardrobe, and found a nice floral Paul Smith shirt with pink delphiniums, tried it on, and decided this shirt will do for today. He made up his mind that he would clear up the mess in his house later, as the thought of running a vacuum cleaner would only make his head throb all the more. He picked up his umbrella and made his way to the front door.

Fifteen minutes later he found himself at the Cuffley Hotel and made a bee-line for the Pompadour Bar, walked to the door and went inside in a nonchalant manner. The bar was already buzzing; everybody turned round and looked at him. Pilchards gave a wry smile, and give two thumbs up to the pubs clientele. Herman the German, a rather large and popular German guy, who worked flipping burgers down at Joes café, took hold of his hand and shook it vigorously, and said: "Congratulations old boy – You must have given your debit card a right good old bashing last night. Vot?"

"I supposed I must have done," said Pilchard. "But it's not every day you turn thirty".

"Yar Yar," said Herman the German, "vot a card you are, in fact the ace of spades, always up for zer good laugh. Nice of you to buy the whole pub a drink last night and to invite them back to your place – Sorry I could not make it as the Fraulein back home tends to hit me over the head with a good German Kochwurst sausage if I get home late. We Germans always have to obey ze orders. Yar Yar. Anyway Svea will be down soon, and she looks radiant, she will be pleased to see you."

"Why?" Pilchard asked

Herman the German , gave Pilchard a hefty punch in the stomach; "Yar, Yar, can't stop playing ze fool Pilchard old chap, but you can't fool me".

Svea Svensson was a good looking Swedish barmaid whom Pilchard Rainham used to chat up, but he did not expect any results as he thought she was out of his league, and moreover the entertainments manager of the pub, a nasty looking brute of a man called Pell (short for Pelham), who was said to have a face that looked like the back of a 242 bus (which many folks claimed was an insult to a 242 bus) had his eyes on her, and Pilchard did not want to be seen as getting in his way.

"Drinks anybody" shouted Pilchard, he had to shout twice as there was some Italian chap Giuseppe Mussolini who was also shouting at the top of his voice, trying to make excuses why his football team had lost yet again.

The Salutary Lesson
and
the Perfect Woman – 3.

Pilchard brought a round of drinks, whilst everybody tried to ignore Giuseppe, who always got loud after a few drinks, and he always had to wave his hands around, so it was best to stay clear of him. He was in full flow as to why the referee had not noticed a blatant handball that had cost his team a penalty, and claimed that someone must have bribed the referee. Herman the German said that might well happen in Italy where the Mafia run things, but not in the good old UK. This got Giuseppe even more agitated, and he proceeded to wave his glass around, spilling half of it on the assembled company and claiming the Germans and the English have no culture. Pilchard just picked up his Snowball and raised it to his lips, when the fearful gargoyle Pell entered the pub – and Pilchard not wishing to upset him said to the barman Steve, "Oh get Pell whatever he wants".

"Don't mind if I do said Pell, a pint of 'AK' please."

Now Pell thought he was a funny man, but it was not just the German who didn't laugh at his jokes but the whole pub.

"I have got a new joke for you all," said Pell and the entire pub groaned as if in pain. "When is a door not a door?"

No one bothered to answer him – So he replied himself; "When it's a Jar, ha ha".

No one smiled and Herman the German said, "Have you pulled your Christmas crackers too early again this year?"

At this Everybody laughed.

"Hold on, Hold on," said Pell. "I have got an even better one".

Giuseppe said, "Well it could not be any worse than your last one".

"Are you all ready for it?" asked Pell.

"As ready as we will ever be," said Herman the German.

"What do you call an Arab in a lift, holding a pint of milk?" Said Pell.

"I don't know," said Pilchard. "What do you call an Arab in a lift holding a pint of Milk?"

"Wait for it, wait for it, folks – A Milk Sheikh."

This joke was met with a stony glum silence.

"Don't you all get it?" said Pell. "Let me explain it's a play on the word Shake and Sheikh".

Herman the German said, "I think our small brains might have just been able to work that out, but some of us might find the joke a tad racist, and why does the Arab have to be in a lift?"

"Ah," said Pell, "do I have to explain everything to you. A lift goes up and down, and would shake the milk see".

"My friendly advice to you is don't give up your daytime job," said our German.

Giuseppe went back to last night's football match, and Herman the German and Pilchard started chatting. After a further ten minutes or so, Svea, came down the stairs into the bar, she looked as pretty as a picture, and as glamorous as any film star. The men in the bar, stood silent for once including Giuseppe, who stopped his commentary of the game halfway through the first half. Somebody wolf whistled, but Svea took no notice and walked up to Pell, and held out her hand to show a diamond engagement ring to him.

"What do you think of that?" she said. "It's a nice rock, don't you think? I got engaged last night".

Pell went all red.

"Who the hell to?" he retorted.

"Why to Pilchard of course. He got down on his knees last night, produced this ring and asked me to marry him. How could I refuse?"

Pilchard turned round on his stool, he could not believe his ears, So that is what happened last night, he got so inebriated, he had proposed to her, and she had accepted.

She turned to Pilchard and said, "I thought you were never going to ask, I love you despite your funny fishy sounding name, after all I am to marry you, not your first name".

She gave him a hot passionate kiss, full on his lips in full view of everybody, and everybody clapped except for Pell who left the pub with his head bowed low.

Steve the Landlord said, "OK, these ones on me. What will it be gentleman and Oh the Future Mrs Rainham?"

MY KINGDOM,
MY KINGDOM,
FOR A HEARING AID – 1.

Mrs Cynthia Mogford looked distressed and worried, and kept on going from room to room in her house and banging doors.

After a while she shouted out to her husband, "has anybody seen my hearing aid, I am sure I put it on the side dresser in the dining room, before I had my bath".

"No," shouted back her husband.

"Well it's not there now, somebody must have moved it," replied Cynthia.

"Don't be silly Cynthia, why in God's name would anybody want to move your hearing aid?" retorted Mr Mogford.

"Look George, stop trying to be funny, and help us find my hearing aid, I am due at the Cuffley residents meeting in less than half an hour."

"You must have made a mistake, you must have placed it elsewhere, or perhaps it has rolled on to the floor," said George. "You know how forgetful you are getting in your dotage".

"Your no spring chicken yourself George," said Cynthia. "Do try and be of some help for once, you have a look on the floor in the dining room, whilst I re-check the house".

"But you said you were sure you placed it on the side dresser in the dining room, so why are you bothering to check the rest of the house?" replied George.

"You know what George, sometimes you can be a right pain in the rectum, sometimes I don't know why I married you, just do as you are told, and go and check the dining room floor will you."

George replied in a low voice, knowing Cynthia could not hear him without her hearing aid, "Yes your majesty".

"What did you say George?"

"I said yes darling."

Five minutes later George came into the bedroom where Cynthia, was still checking the bed sheets for her hearing aid.

"Cynthia," said George, but she did not hear him, so he tapped her on the shoulder. Cynthia turned around with a jump.

"What do you want to do that for, you scared the life out of me, you could have been a burglar or a rapist."

"Not unless the rapist carried a white stick and had a guide dog. Rapist; you should be so lucky you old trout," replied George.

Cynthia did not respond to Georges goading, perhaps she did not hear him, who knows!

"Cynthia stop your looking, I have found your hearing aid, it must have rolled on to the floor, when you placed it on the dining room table." George held up the hearing aid – it was in bits.

"What happened?" cried Cynthia.

"I trod on it whilst scanning the floor," said George.

"You clumsy oaf, now I will have to go to the residents meeting without my hearing aid."

Mrs Cynthia Mogford was late for the meeting in the village hall, She burst in, saying, "sorry I am late, but I have not got my hearing aid in tonight, it's broken".

The chairman Mr Tim Bellingham said, "Sorry I did not catch that, my batteries appear to have gone dead in my hearing aid – we were going to start the meeting without you".

Burt Fleecum turned to fellow committee member Audrey Willmott, and said; "Looks like the meeting could be fun tonight".

"What was that you said?" said Tom Barks "Missed what you are saying, left my hearing aid at home tonight by mistake".

"Ah gawd – My Giddy Aunt – three of them without their hearing aids," said Burt Fleecum.

The Chairman, Tim Bellingham, opened the meeting with apologise for absence – and Tom Barks, put his hand up, "Yes Tom what is it?"

"I have some sad news to report Beryl Murphy is no longer with us," said Tom.

Tim Bellingham said, "what did he say – he will have to speak up, can't hear him, in fact everybody will have to speak up."

Burt Fleecum said, "he should have brought his ear mufflers to the meeting".

Whilst Cynthia Mogford shouted to the chairman, "I think he said Beryl Murphy has passed away".

My Kingdom
My Kingdom,
For a Hearing Aid – 2.

"Come again," said Tom Barks.

"Oh," said the Chairman Tim Bellingham. "Sorry to hear that, this is indeed shock news, I understood that although she was over seventy she was in rude health, was it a heart attack and when did this happen?"

Tom Barks said, "say again, I did not quite catch what the chairman just said".

"Pardon," said Cynthia Mogford, "what did Tom just say?"

Tom Barks said, "At half past eight".

And Cynthia replied, "What?"

Tom said, "Didn't somebody just ask about when it happened?"

"Did what happen?" said Cynthia?

"We were talking Beryl Murphy, it happened at eight thirty pm last Monday," said Tom.

"Oh," said the chairman, "Beryl's husband Jim, must be beside himself, I understand they have been together for over fifty years, he must be upset, and we will have to let everybody know, so that they can send flowers and condolence cards and notes".

"What did he just say?" said Tom, "didn't catch a word of that, the chairman needs to shout louder".

Bert Fleecum interjected and spoke slowly with a loud clear voice to Tom, "the Chairman just said Beryl's husband Jim must be beside himself and upset".

Tom said, "well he would be, if that had happened to your wife, just think of all the extra work load for him with Beryl out of the picture".

The Chairman said, "Beryl has been a committee member of this Cuffley residents group for about a decade and I think it's only right that we as an association should send a bunch of flowers, after all the hard work she has put in over the years".

The chairman looked across at the treasurer, and continued, "I feel sure our funds could stretch to that".

The treasurer nodded in agreement.

"I therefore propose that we go ahead with that, do I have a seconder?"

Tom Barks put his hand up and a vote was taken, and they unanimously agreed that the flowers should be ordered forthwith.

The rest of the meeting proceeded as usual, with the normal list of subjects from dog poo on the playing fields with Audrey Willmot objecting to the word poo and putting in a motion that the minutes should record the words dog 'Faeces' not poo.

Other subjects discussed were speeding traffic, pot-holes, children riding bikes on the pavement without using a bell, and the gaudy colour on the front of a big house on the Ridgeway

After every subject was dissected in minute detail Audrey Willmot said, "that her life had been ruined and that it should not be allowed".

Burt Fleecum kept on looking at his watch, as the meeting was dragging on, and he wanted to get to the pub before last orders.

At long last the Chairman Tim Bellingham said, "Any other business?"

"I hope not said Burt".

But Tom Barks put his hand up, "I have something further to report".

And Burt said, "Not more bad news I hope?"

"No," said Tom. "Just that me and the memsahib are going on a Saga tour down to Bournemouth for a month, and we're leaving by coach first thing in the morning, so depending what time we come back, I may have to miss next month's meeting or be late for the meeting".

Burt said, "Bournemouth? Don't you mean bath chair city ha ha?"

And Tom retorted; "Did you not listen? I said Bournemouth not Bath. Went to Bath last year I told you so at the last meeting, nice as it is why would I want to go to the same place twice?"

Burt said, "Oh I give up ".

The chairman said at long last I declare this meeting closed.

My Kingdom,
My Kingdom
for a Hearing Aid – 3.

The news of Beryl Murphy's untimely demise was soon disseminated via the good folk of Cuffley's Residents Association and within hours the local village jungle drums, had brought the sad news to almost everybody living in Cuffley including the out laying farms.

The next few days saw Jim Murphy's house almost inundated with cards of condolences, sorry to hear cards, letters and at least three funeral wreaths. A large number of flowers were sent and by far the largest bunch of flowers was a massive display sent by Cuffley Residents Association. 'Cut and Dried' the local florist, had never worked so hard in twenty years and were grateful for the extra work put their way. Many of the letters and cards, asked when and where the funeral was going to take place, as many folk pledged to come, as Beryl had been around some time, and indeed had taught at Cuffley Primary School, when she first got married it seemed that Beryl, was part of the fixtures and fittings of the place, and was an integral part of its ethos.

Scroll on a month to the start of the next residents meeting, and we can picture them all talking away,

without Tom Barks, who must have been held up returning from his trip down to Bournemouth. After the
meeting had been in full flow for about half an hour,
Tom Barks strolled in saying, "sorry I am late, coach got
held up due to an accident on the M25, but the good
news I have my hearing aid in tonight".

There was a stony silence; you could hear a pin drop
as everybody gazed at Tom intently.

After a while Tom said, "what's up, have I done
something wrong? I am late and I have already apolo-
gized for that".

"You knows what's up," said the Chairman Tim
Bellingham. "You and your sick sense of humour, I
suppose you were laughing all the way down to
Bournemouth and back, you have brought Cuffley
Residents Association into disrepute and don't know
how you dare to show your face here".

"What have I done?" asked Tom.

"As if you don't know," said the chairman.

"I don't know," said Tom, "I really don't know,
please enlighten me".

Tim Bellingham face went red with anger as he stood
and shouted across the assembled members.

"Ok let me spell it out to you – you said Beryl was
dead, and we told the entire village, but she was not
dead, only laid up in bed with a slip disc. We sent
flowers, and we had a most annoyed Jim Murphy on
the phone threatening to sue us for libel and slander as
his wife is still very much alive and kicking".

"I never said she was dead," said Tom.

"Oh yes you did, everybody here heard you – you
said Beryl is no longer with us and you even seconded a
motion to send Flowers".

Tom replied; "That's right I spoke to Beryl that very morning on the phone and she said that due to her bad back and her age, she felt it was time for her to retire from our residents group whilst she was still at the top – and that's what I reported to you. When you asked for apologies for absence, I replied correctly that Beryl will no longer be with us, and of course we should send her flowers, what with her bad back, and all the work she has done for us in the past".

No one said a word for what seemed like ages. Then Burt Fleecum broke out in fits of laughter, and after a couple of minutes he got up from the table and said; "Excuse me Ladies and Gents, must go to the big boys powder room, I think I am going to wet my pants!"

THE NOT SO WILD, 'WILD BUNCH' – 1.

L.P. Hartley famously wrote in his book *The Go-Between* that the past is a foreign country. For folk who were born between the two world wars, this quote no doubt has a ring of truth to it. Britain was a very different country then, the empire was still *in situ*, and religion was enmeshed into the everyday life of the populous. Our values (Some good, some bad), have changed to such an extent, that children brought up in the 1920s and 1930s could have not contemplated todays values and mores (some good and some bad). However most of our older population have adjusted their views over a period of time to reflect a more liberal world. But some other folk, have found themselves stuck in a rut of the past and have refused to move on. They are just part of the cultural residue of a bygone age. One such person was Miss Gladys Pure, a Spinster of the Parish, who considered herself a virtuous person, a pillar of the community, and the one person in the Parish that could still up hold the old values.

Burt Fleecum (you remember him from the last story) was born after the war, and was the editor of the local paper, which had a letters column. A column which Miss Pure took a great dislike to. She found the paper was amoral, and did not promote her interpretation of Christian values although the paper gave widespread coverage to church events. One day in pursuit of her personal moral crusade, Burt found her hiding behind the village letterbox with her head poking out, looking at something up the road. Burt approached her and asked her politely what she was looking at, and if there was a problem.

Gladys Pure replied, "There was a black man taking cardboard boxes into a house up the road".

Burt said, "Ah – That's the local solicitor Mr Coffee Okonjo moving into his new house".

But all our Gladys Pure said was, "Oh but he is black and taking boxes into that house I must keep an eye on him".

At this point Miss Pure decided she could get a better view of him, if she crossed the road and hid behind a tree by the old Telephone exchange.

It was whilst hiding there, that the police arrested her as some kind of geriatric Peeping Tom. The Police did not hold her for long, after she explained what she was doing. She was upset a great deal at been told off, by such a young policeman, and asked who reported that she was hiding in the bush, was it Burt Fleecum?

The policeman could not confirm who reported her (and for the record it was not Burt Fleecum). But Gladys Pure was not sure she believed him. What Miss Pure expected to view is not clear, maybe she thought, that smuggled diamonds, drugs, or stolen silver plate, or even weapons were going to drop out of Mr Okonjo cardboard boxes, who knows?

About a year later the local Vicar the Rev John Ale got a phone call from a much distressed Gladys Pure, "It's that Burt Fleecum," she said.

"I am disgusted and offended," said Miss Pure.

The Vicar said, "what has he done now to upset you, it must have been something really bad?"

"It's the local paper. I am deeply offended and mortally wounded by his personal offensive comments".

"So what has he actually said?" retorted the Rev John Ale.

"It's the nickname column in the paper, we are called the wild bunch, and the last of the summer wine crew, a clear reference to the Parish Council, and members of the church".

"What do you expect me to do said the Vicar?"

"Well Burt Fleecum is a member of our church and our congregation, can't you ban him from church or something?"

"Not sure I can do that Miss Pure".

"Now look here Vicar, you have got to do something about this, can't have church members going around insulting other churchgoers can we, so what are you going to do about it?"

"Leave it with me Miss Pure, let me think about it, and I can assure you some actions will be taken to resolve the problem."

THE NOT SO WILD 'WILD BUNCH' – 2.

" Thank you Vicar for seeing sense – good night Vicar," she then slammed down the phone.

A week later the Rev John Ale, spoke to Burt Fleecum after the morning church service and Holy Communion. "Excuse me Burt, have you got a moment, can I have a word in your ear".

"Sure no problem," said Burt.

"I need to speak to you as a matter of urgency," said the Vicar.

"Well you can speak to me now," said Burt.

"I would rather not," said the Vicar.

"Well where and when do you wish to speak to me?" replied Burt.

"How about at The Plough public house after the service if that is convenient with you?" said the Vicar

"You mean opposite The Plough on the bench next to the village pump?"

"No," said the Vicar, "I was thinking more about the inside of the pub, we should be able to find a quiet secluded table away from the bar, if that's OK with you".

"Fine," said Burt, "no problem".

Well our Vicar and the chief protagonist meet up at The Plough as agreed.

The Vicar sat down, with a solemn face and started to talk, "Burt you have caused me a great deal of grief, and I have had to spend the entire day with the Bishop of Hertford discussing you. Bishops are very busy men you understand, and you have interrupted the smooth running of the church."

Burt tried to speak, but the Vicar held up his hand. "Please do the courtesy of letting me finish – you have insulted members of my congregation in public – and I have asked the Bishop if we can ban you from church. We can't find anything in Church Law that allows us to do that, however although we can't ban you from church we have found a little known rule that goes back to 1785 or was it 1875, (Vicar fumbles around in his pocket) I have it written down somewhere on a sheet of paper for you to see, if I can find it, that allows us to ban you from taking the Holy Eucharist, if you don't publicly apologise and mend your evil ways".

"So what have I said?" said Burt.

"As you well know, you called, members of my church 'the Wild Bunch' and the 'Last of the Summer Wine Crew'".

Burt burst out laughing and the Vicar said, "I am being serious and really can ban you, you seem to treat these insults in a flippant manor and you really don't do your case any good by your attitude".

Burt put his hands on the Vicars shoulder and said; "Please turn around, see that group of mature men drinking at the bar, they are all in their seventies and eighties, and they met up once a week on a Sunday lunchtime for a drink".

'What of it – what has this to do with your insults?" said the Vicar.

"Well go and ask them what the nickname for their group is, and what they call themselves".

The Rev John Ale went as white as a sheet. "Oh I have been barking up the wrong street – and yes that is very funny".

"Shall we leave it at that Vicar?" said Burt.

At this the Vicar got up and left. Shortly after this the Vicar announced he was going to retire, and Burt ceased to be a regular in church, so that Gladys got her own way in the end.

Moral of this story – One churchgoer with extreme antediluvian attitudes can undo the hard work of one hundred churchgoers. And the church should always try to remember that the real public face of the church is not the clergy, but the worshipers.

THE LOST UNDERPANTS – 1.

Older readers can no doubt recall the UK miners' strike from 1984–85. For many it was seen as a battle between the Conservatives under Mrs Thatcher, and the NUM (The National Union of Mineworkers) under Arthur Scargill. The country appeared to be unstable, and tempers were running high on both sides of the debate. Things were turning nasty 'Up North' as the police had to do battle with striking mineworkers and 'Flying pickets'. As a result of the conflict, police officers from the Metropolitan police were seconded, to help out their battered northern colleagues. This is where our story begins.

Burt Fleecum received a phone call from his chum, Nigel Pomfrett, a serving officer in the Metropolitan police force.

"Morning Burt," said Nigel, "I wonder if you can help me out with a little problem".

"Well it depends what it is and how little it is," said Burt.

"Well it's a little delicate," replied Nigel, "remember I said I was due to go up north because of the miners strike?"

Yes you told me last week, what of it?"

"Well the Met police have supplied us with special blue issue underpants for the duration – and well last night I had a tad too much to drink and I think my curry was off – and one thing led to another if you get my drift."

"Do you mean to say you did a number two in your pants Nigel?"

"Yes I did, but I did not want my wife to see, dare not chuck it away in the bin, so this morning I drove just outside the Parish and chucked them over a hedge down 'Silver Street'."

Burt laughed and said, "Ah police getting rid of the evidence again, but what has this to do with me?"

"Well I need to retrieve my underpants, and I need you to help me."

"Why in God's name do you want to retrieve your underpants?"

"Well unbeknown to me, my darling wife had sewn my name and address into the pants, and I can't risk somebody finding them and returning them."

"I thought that only mothers did that to their infant children, not wives of grown up men," Said Burt in reply.

Nigel sighed and said, "She was only doing what she thought was best for me."

And Burt said, "did you not notice, the label when you put your underpants on, or when you took them off?"

Nigel was getting a tad annoyed with Burt and went on, "it was dark, when I put the pants on, did not want to turn on the light and wake the wife, and any rate, why would I be looking for a label in the first place, I bet you don't check for labels in your underpants before you put them on, anyway it's all water under the bridge now".

And Burt said, "or pants over the hedgerow ha ha".

This remark did not solicit a laugh from Nigel, who just said, "Well are you going to help me, or not?"

"Of course I will help you," said Burt.

"Great," said Nigel, "pick you up in ten minutes,"

Our two intrepid underpants seekers drove out of the Parish to Silver Street, but found the road and the surrounding area covered in a low dense fog.

"Just which hedge did you chuck them over?" said Burt.

"Not sure," replied Nigel, "it was dark when I did it, and this dense fog has caused me to lose my bearings."

"That's not much of a help," said Burt, "so let's start from basics, was it the right hand side of this country lane, or the left hand side?"

"Oh that's easy, it was the right hand side I am sure."

Burt said, "this lane must be a couple of miles long, I need more details of the hedge if we are ever going to find your pants, was it before or after the deserted old army barracks?"

There was a pause before Nigel spoke again.

"It was after the old army barracks."

The lost underpants – 2.

"I think..." Burt said.

"You think, but you are not sure, that's a great help."

"I am 99 percent certain it was after the army barracks."

"Fine," said Burt, "now, you are the detective, you tell us where we should start looking".

"We will just have to try every hedge along this road, my pants can't be that hard to find."

At this point in the story Burt, put his flat hand to his forehead and proclaimed that he felt sure Doctor Watson did not have this problem with Sherlock Holmes.

Two hours later, they still had not recovered Nigel's underpants, and the fog had lifted only to be replaced by a heavy drizzle, which was rapidly soaking into our hero's clothes.

At long last Nigel said, "I think we should give up now, my bet is that some animal, like a fox or a badger has dragged the pants off to their nest."

And Burt said, "Yep I am sure some male badger said to himself, 'Oh look soiled underpants, must take them home to Mrs Badger in her set, she will be impressed'".

Six months later Nigel was back with his wife, eating his breakfast, which consisted of Kellogg's Sugar

Frosties, and black coffee. He had forgotten all about his lost pants, and looked forward to the meeting of the local temperance league, which he had joined after his last big drink up in the local village hall on that fateful evening.

Then there was a knock at the door, and Mrs Pomfrett, said to Nigel, 'don't get up, I will get it, you finish your breakfast".

Mrs Pomfrett returned and handed Nigel a small package whilst saying, "it's address to you, perhaps it's that book you ordered on flower arranging last week".

Nigel opened the package, and his jaw dropped as what greeted his eyes were none other than his underpants. Nigel looked like he had just been stabbed by a red-hot poker, and Mrs Pomfrett noticed that there was a note left in the paper packaging.

She picked it up and read it out loud, "I herewith return your underpants as requested, from where you left them in that field. I have taken the liberty of sending them to the laundry before I posted them back to you, hope you don't mind – yours Love Sally".

"Who the hell is Sally?" she shouted at Nigel, "so that is what you got up to whilst up north?"

Nigel could not answer, other than to say he had no idea who she was, and that he had not been up to nothing up north, and asked her to check the postmark.

Mrs Pomfrett checked the postmark, and it was posted locally. "Ah so it's a local girl, you are seeing behind my back then?"

"No, I have not," said Nigel.

"Then how do you explain this note?" said Mrs P. And of course he could not explain it.

Two weeks later Nigel, came home after work, only to find his wife was not there, and a note saying she had gone back to live with her mother – divorce papers would follow in the post

UPMARKET – 1.

Some years back The Plough Public house got a new governor. This new landlord said to his wife, "look at the houses up The Ridgway, some of them must be worth millions, and who do we get drinking here, nothing but the dross of Cuffley? We don't need the people from the poor end of Cuffley like Station Road, or the council house end of Tolmers Road, by the scout camp. What we need to do is go 'upmarket', believe you me there are to be changes round here when l take over next week. We need to attract the gin and tonic brigade, not the pints of AK scum".

His wife said, "what do you intend to do?"

"For a start we should have a dress code, tuxedos, or a suit and tie for men and for woman, a proper dress, no jeans and so forth."

The opening night for the new Landlord was a Saturday, and our new governor turned everybody away, as their dress sense was not up to his standard. His wife asked if this was a wise move, and he replied, "Don't worry they will soon get the message, and folks will be flocking to this place, and we will make a fortune."

In the meantime, the Cuffley Hotel was packed full of Plough refugees, all with a story to tell. The local gamekeeper, saying that he had drunk in The Plough for thirty years, and he had never been refused a drink before, and the same was said by Mr Ken Smith who owned a local plumbing and electrical supply store. Whilst both Lord and Lady Cuffley were fuming with rage. Lord Cuffley told the bar that The Plough's new landlord, has told him that he ran a, "respectable joint" and could not let scruffy people like him and his good lady wife in.

"Blooming cheek of the man and not only that," he went on, "I asked if the wife could use his convenience as she had to powder her nose and you know what the blighter said? No you can't, and any way your hair is too long. I asked him what in the name of god, has the length of my hair got to with not allowing my wife to use the loo? He then told me to Bugger off and go home."

A Banker turned round and said, "I work in the city all week, and have to be smart and wear a suit and tie at all times. My weekends are my knocking off period, and yet I am told by that idiot up the road, I can't come in without a suit and tie".

Last to turn up was the General, "What are you doing here?" said Burt Fleecum. "You normally fre-quent The Plough as your usual watering hole, he can't have banned you, as you always look immaculate".

"Sorry chaps," said the general it appears I am in the same boat as you, pulled up in my old jalopy, and that new chap, said it lowers the tone of the place, told me to park round the back or over the road. I told the bounder he could stuff his beer, so I sort of banned myself".

"Good on you general," said the local builder, "too bloody right".

Burt Fleecum said, "I have got an idea to stop this new chap in his tracks, but it might take a few days to put together".

Our ex-Plough drinkers huddled around Burt and starting talking in low whispers, and every now and again, they burst out with hoots of laughter. After some time, Burt was heard to say, "Well that's settled lads, we are all agreed, let's get to work on project".

Next Saturday the new Landlord of The Plough was woken up by a commotion outside the front of his establishment, and pandemonium seemed to have broken out. There was a large crowd; a BBC camera crew and the local press were in attendance. Our new landlord could not make out what was going on, so he rushed out front demanding an explanation for the racket.

Upmarket – 2.

The new landlord barged his way through the crowd, and could not understand why everybody was pointing and laughing at him. He reached the centre of the crowd, and almost had a heart attack. Somebody had cemented a lavatory to the ground in his front car park, with a dead Badger sitting on it, pulling the chain. Next to it somebody had also cemented a signpost pointing at The Plough saying 'Public Toilet'. The landlord shouted out, "You bastards" and ran back into the pub.

Needless to say he was gone within a week!

www.ingramcontent.com/pod-product-compliance
Lightning Source LLC
Chambersburg PA
CBHW020344130626
46549CB00003B/1286